P9-DMB-268

DOVER · THRIFT · EDITIONS

Oedipus Rex

SOPHOCLES

DOVER PUBLICATIONS, INC.
New York

DOVER THRIFT EDITIONS

EDITOR: STANLEY APPELBAUM

Published in Canada by General Publishing Company, Ltd., 30 Lesmill Road, Don Mills, Toronto, Ontario.
Published in the United Kingdom by Constable and Company, Ltd., 3 The Lanchesters, 162–164 Fulham Palace Road, London W6 9ER.

This Dover edition, first published in 1991, is an unabridged republication of the play *Oedipus Tyrannus* from the volume *The Dramas of Sophocles Rendered in English Verse Dramatic & Lyric by Sir George Young,* as published by J. M. Dent & Sons, Ltd., London, in 1906. (The Dent edition was the second, the first having been published by George Bell & Sons, London, in 1888.) See the new Note, specially written for the Dover edition, for further details.

Manufactured in the United States of America
Dover Publications, Inc.,
31 East 2nd Street,
Mineola, N.Y. 11501

Library of Congress Cataloging-in-Publication Data

Sophocles.
[Oedipus Rex. English]
Oedipus Rex / Sophocles.
p. cm. — (Dover thrift editions)
Unabridged republication of the play Oedipus rendered in English verse by Sir George Young, published by J.M. Dent, London, 1906.
ISBN 0-486-26877-2
1. Oedipus (Greek mythology)—Drama. I. Young, George, Sir, 1837–1930. II. Title. III. Series.
PA4414.O7Y68 1991
882′.01—dc20 91-9464
CIP

Note

SOPHOCLES (born ca. 496 B.C., died after 413) was one of the three major authors of Greek tragedy. Of his 123 plays, only seven survive in full. We are fortunate that one of these is *Oedipus Rex* (in Greek, *Oidipous tyrannos*), written soon after 430 B.C., which the ancient Greeks themselves considered his best work.

Still exciting to read or see, *Oedipus Rex* is famous for its smooth and suspenseful plotting, its cosmic ironies and the philosophical questions it raises about the limits of man's power and ambitions. (Note: *Antigone, Oedipus Rex* and *Oedipus at Colonus* were written many years apart, and do not form a trilogy.)

The translation by Sir George Young (1837–1930; he called it *Oedipus Tyrannus*) is not only very accurate; it also preserves the feeling of the original Greek to a great extent. The verse forms are reasonable English equivalents; the diction—lightly archaic in the blank-verse dialogues, heightened and more involuted in the stanzaic choruses—admirably reflects the hieratic nature of Sophocles' drama.

In the present edition, Sir George's own notes (exclusively concerned with problems of the Greek text and its interpretation) have been omitted. Several new, very brief footnotes have been added, identifying some Greek terms and concepts for readers less familiar with classical mythology and lore.

Persons Represented

OEDIPUS, *King of Thebes.*

PRIEST *of Zeus.*

CREON, *brother to Jocasta the Queen.*

TIRESIAS, *a Prophet, with the title of King.*

A Messenger from Corinth.

An old Shepherd.

A Second Messenger, servant of Oedipus' household.

JOCASTA *the Queen, wife to Oedipus, formerly married to Laius, the last King.*

ANTIGONE, ISMENE, } *daughters to Oedipus and Jocasta.*

The CHORUS *is composed of Senators of Thebes.*

Inhabitants of Thebes, Attendants.

A Boy leading Tiresias.

Oedipus Rex

Scene, before the Royal Palace at Thebes. Enter OEDIPUS; *to him the Priest of Zeus, and Inhabitants of Thebes.*

OEDIPUS Children, you modern brood of Cadmus* old,
What mean you, sitting in your sessions here,
High-coronalled with votive olive-boughs,
While the whole city teems with incense-smoke,
And paean hymns, and sounds of woe the while?
Deeming unmeet, my children, this to learn
From others, by the mouth of messengers,
I have myself come hither, Oedipus,
Known far and wide by name. Do thou, old man,
Since 'tis thy privilege to speak for these,
Say in what case ye stand; if of alarm,
Or satisfaction with my readiness
To afford all aid; hard-hearted must I be,
Did I not pity such petitioners.

PRIEST Great Oedipus, my country's governor,
Thou seest our generations, who besiege
Thy altars here; some not yet strong enough
To flutter far; some priests, with weight of years
Heavy, myself of Zeus; and these, the flower
Of our young manhood; all the other folk
Sit, with like branches, in the market-place,

* Founder of Thebes.

By the Ismenian hearth oracular*
And the twin shrines of Pallas.** Lo, the city
Labours—thyself art witness—over-deep
Already, powerless to uprear her head
Out of the abysses of a surge of blood;
Stricken in the budding harvest of her soil,
Stricken in her pastured herds, and barren travail
Of women; and He, the God with spear of fire,
Leaps on the city, a cruel pestilence,
And harries it; whereby the Cadmean home
Is all dispeopled, and with groan and wail
The blackness of the Grave made opulent.
Not that we count thee as the peer of Heaven,
I, nor these children, seat us at thy hearth;
But as of men found foremost in affairs,
Chances of life and shifts of Providence;
Whose coming to our Cadmean town released
The toll we paid, of a hard Sorceress,***
And that, without instruction or advice
Of our imparting; but of Heaven it came
Thou art named, and known, our life's establisher.
Thee therefore, Oedipus, the mightiest head
Among us all, all we thy supplicants
Implore to find some way to succour us,
Whether thou knowest it through some voice from heaven,
Or, haply of some man; for I perceive
In men experienced that their counsels best
Find correspondence in things actual.
Haste thee, most absolute sir, be the state's builder!
Haste thee, look to it; doth not our country now
Call thee deliverer, for thy zeal of yore?
Never let us remember of thy rule

* Referring to Ismene, a legendary Theban woman.
** Athena.
*** The Sphinx, whose riddle Oedipus guessed.

That we stood once erectly, and then fell;
But build this city in stability!
With a fair augury didst thou shape for us
Our fortune then; like be thy prowess now!
If thou wilt rule this land (which thou art lord of),
It were a fairer lordship filled with folk
Than empty; towers and ships are nothingness,
Void of our fellow men to inhabit them.

OEDIPUS Ah my poor children, what you come to seek
Is known already—not unknown to me.
You are all sick, I know it; and in your sickness
There is not one of you so sick as I.
For in your case his own particular pain
Comes to each singly; but my heart at once
Groans for the city, and for myself, and you.
Not therefore as one taking rest in sleep
Do you uprouse me; rather deem of me
As one that wept often, and often came
By many ways through labyrinths of care;
And the one remedy that I could find
By careful seeking—I supplied it. Creon,
Menoeceus' son, the brother of my queen,
I sent to Pytho, to Apollo's house,
To ask him by what act or word of mine
I might redeem this city; and the hours
Already measured even with today
Make me solicitous how he has sped;
For he is longer absent than the time
Sufficient, which is strange. When he shall come,
I were a wretch did I not then do all
As the God shews.

PRIEST In happy time thou speak'st;
As these, who tell me Creon is at hand.

OEDIPUS Ah King Apollo, might he but bring grace,
Radiant in fortune, as he is in face!

PRIEST I think he comes with cheer; he would not, else,

Thus be approaching us with crown on brow,
All berries of the bay.

OEDIPUS We shall know soon;
He is within hearing.

Enter CREON, *attended.*

My good lord and cousin,
Son of Menoeceus,
What answer of the God have you brought home?

CREON Favourable; I mean, even what sounds ominously,
If it have issue in the way forthright,
May all end well.

OEDIPUS How runs the oracle?
I am not confident, nor prone to fear
At what you say, so far.

CREON If you desire
To hear while these stand near us, I am ready
To speak at once—or to go in with you.

OEDIPUS Speak before all! My heavy load of care
More for their sake than for my own I bear.

CREON What the God told me, that will I declare.
Phoebus our Lord gives us express command
To drive pollution, bred within this land,
Out of the country, and not cherish it
Beyond the power of healing.

OEDIPUS By what purge?
What is the tenor of your tragedy?

CREON Exile, or recompense of death for death;
Since 'tis this blood makes winter to the city.

OEDIPUS Whose fate is this he signifies?

CREON My liege,
We had a leader, once, over this land,
Called Laius—ere you held the helm of state.

OEDIPUS So I did hear; I never saw the man.

CREON The man is dead; and now, we are clearly bidden
To bring to account certain his murderers.

Oedipus is sincerely trying to figure out who killed Laius, unknowing that he was Laius' murderer

OEDIPUS And where on earth are they? Where shall be found
This dim-seen track-mark of an ancient crime?

CREON "Within this land," it ran. That which is sought,
That may be caught. What is unheeded scapes us.

OEDIPUS Was it at home, afield, or anywhere
Abroad, that Laius met this violent end?

CREON He went professedly on pilgrimage;
But since he started, came back home no more.

OEDIPUS Nor any messenger nor way-fellow
Looked on, from whom one might have learnt his story
And used it?

CREON No, they perished, all but one;
He fled, affrighted; and of what he saw
Had but one thing to say for certain.

OEDIPUS Well,
And what was that? one thing might be the means
Of our discovering many, could we gain
Some narrow ground for hope.

CREON Robbers, he said,
Met them, and slew him; by no single strength,
But multitude of hands.

OEDIPUS How could your robber
Have dared so far—except there were some practice
With gold from hence?

CREON Why, it seemed probable.
But, Laius dead, no man stood up to help
Amid our ills.

OEDIPUS What ill was in the way,
Which, when a sovereignty had lapsed like this,
Kept you from searching of it out?

CREON The Sphinx
With her enigma forced us to dismiss
Things out of sight, and look to our own steps.

OEDIPUS Well, I will have it all to light again.
Right well did Phoebus, yea and well may you
Insist on this observance toward the dead;

So shall you see me, as of right, with you,
Venging this country and the God together.
Why, 'tis not for my neighbours' sake, but mine,
I shall dispel this plague-spot; for the man,
Whoever it may be, who murdered him,
Lightly might hanker to serve me the same.
I benefit myself in aiding him.
Up then, my children, straightway, from the floor;
Take up your votive branches; let some other
Gather the tribes of Cadmus hitherward;
Say, I will make clean work. Please Heaven, our state
Shall soon appear happy, or desperate.

PRIEST Come children, let us rise; it was for this,
Which he himself proclaims, that we came hither.
Now may the sender of these oracles,
In saving and in plague-staying, Phoebus, come!

[*Exeunt* CREON, PRIEST *and* THEBANS.
OEDIPUS *retires*.

Enter THEBAN SENATORS, *as Chorus*.

Chorus.

I. 1.

O Prophecy of Jove, whose words are sweet,
With what doom art thou sent
To glorious Thebes, from Pytho's gilded seat?
I am distraught with fearful wonderment,
I thrill with terror, and wait reverently—
Yea, Io Paean, Delian lord,* on thee!
What matter thou wilt compass—either strange,
Or once again recurrent as the seasons change,
Offspring of golden Hope, immortal Oracle,
Tell me, O tell!

* Apollo.

I. 2.

Athena first I greet with invocation,
Daughter of Jove, divine!
Next Artemis thy sister, of this nation
Keeper, high seated in the encircling shrine,
Filled with her praises, of our market-place,
And Phoebus, shooting arrows far through space;
Appear ye Three, the averters of my fate!
If e'er before, when mischief rose upon the state,
Ye quenched the flames of evil, putting them away,
Come—come to-day!

II. 1.

Woe, for unnumbered are the ills we bear!
Sickness pervades our hosts;
Nor is there any spear of guardian care,
Wherewith a man might save us, found in all our
coasts.
For all the fair soil's produce now no longer springs;
Nor women from the labour and loud cries
Of their child-births arise;
And you may see, flying like a bird with wings,
One after one, outspeeding the resistless brand,
Pass—to the Evening Land.

II. 2.

In countless hosts our city perisheth.
Her children on the plain
Lie all unpitied—pitiless—breeding death.
Our wives meanwhile, and white-haired mothers in
their train,
This way and that, suppliant, along the altar-side
Sit, and bemoan their doleful maladies;
Like flame their paeans rise,
With wailing and lament accompanied;

For whose dear sake O Goddess, O Jove's golden child,
Send Help with favour mild!

III. 1.

And Ares the Destroyer, him who thus—
Not now in harness of brass shields, as wont—
Ringed round with clamour, meets us front to front
And fevers us,
O banish from our country! Drive him back,
With winds upon his track,
On to the chamber vast of Amphitrite,*
Or that lone anchorage, the Thracian main;
For now, if night leave bounds to our annoy,
Day levels all again;
Wherefore, O father, Zeus, thou that dost wield the
    might
Of fire-fraught light,
Him with thy bolt destroy!

III. 2.

Next, from the bendings of thy golden string
I would see showered thy artillery
Invincible, marshalled to succour me,
Lycean King!**
Next, those flame-bearing beams, arrows most bright,
Which Artemis by night
Through Lycian highlands speeds her scattering;
Thou too, the Evian, with thy Maenad band,
Thou golden-braided patron of this land
Whose visage glows with wine,
O save us from the god whom no gods honour! Hear,
Bacchus! Draw near,
And light thy torch of pine!

Enter OEDIPUS, *attended.*

* The sea.
** Apollo.

OEDIPUS You are at prayers; but for your prayers' intent
You may gain help, and of your ills relief,
If you will minister to the pestilence,
And hearken and receive my words, which I—
A stranger to this tale, and to the deed
A stranger—shall pronounce; for of myself
I could not follow up the traces far,
Not having any key. But, made since then
A fellow-townsman to the townsmen here,
To all you Cadmeans I thus proclaim;
Whichever of you knows the man, by whom
Laius the son of Labdacus was slain,
Even if he is afraid, seeing he himself
Suppressed the facts that made against himself,
I bid that man shew the whole truth to me;
For he shall suffer no disparagement,
Except to quit the land, unscathed. Again,
If any knows another—say some stranger
To have been guilty, let him not keep silence;
For I will pay him the reward, and favour
Shall be his due beside it. But again,
If you will hold your peace, and any man
From self or friend in terror shall repel
This word of mine, then—you must hear me say
What I shall do. Whoe'er he be, I order
That of this land, whose power and throne are mine,
None entertain him, none accost him, none
Cause him to share in prayers or sacrifice
Offered to Heaven, or pour him lustral wave,
But all men from their houses banish him;
Since it is he contaminates us all,
Even as the Pythian oracle divine
Revealed but now to me. Such is my succour
Of him that's dead, and of the Deity.
And on the guilty head I imprecate
That whether by himself he has lain covert,
Or joined with others, without happiness,

Evil, in evil, he may pine and die.
And for myself I pray, if with my knowledge
He should become an inmate of my dwelling,
That I may suffer all that I invoked
On these just now. Moreover all these things
I charge you to accomplish, in behalf
Of me, and of the God, and of this land,
So ruined, barren and forsaken of Heaven.
For even though the matter were not now
By Heaven enjoined you, 'twas unnatural
For you to suffer it to pass uncleansed,
A man most noble having been slain, a king too!
Rather, you should have searched it out; but now,
Since I am vested with the government
Which he held once, and have his marriage-bed,
And the same wife; and since our progeny—
If his had not miscarried—had sprung from us
With common ties of common motherhood—
Only that Fate came heavy upon his head—
On these accounts I, as for my own father,
Will fight this fight, and follow out every clue,
Seeking to seize the author of his murder—
The scion of Labdacus and Polydore
And earlier Cadmus and Agenor old;
And such as disobey—the Gods I ask
Neither to raise them harvest from the ground
Nor children from the womb, but that they perish
By this fate present, and yet worse than this;
While you, the other Cadmeans, who approve,
May succouring Justice and all Gods in heaven
Accompany for good for evermore!

1 SENATOR Even as thou didst adjure me, so, my king,
I will reply. I neither murdered him,
Nor can point out the murderer. For the quest—
To tell us who on earth has done this deed
Belonged to Phoebus, by whose word it came.

OEDIPUS Your words are just; but to constrain the Gods
To what they will not, passes all men's power.
1 SENATOR I would say something which appears to me
The second chance to this.
OEDIPUS And your third, also—
If such you have—by all means tell it.
1 SENATOR Sir,
Tiresias above all men, I am sure,
Ranks as a seer next Phoebus, king with king;
Of him we might enquire and learn the truth
With all assurance.
OEDIPUS That is what I did;
And with no slackness; for by Creon's advice
I sent, twice over; and for some time, now,
'Tis strange he is not here.
1 SENATOR Then all the rest
Are but stale words and dumb.
OEDIPUS What sort of words?
I am weighing every utterance.
1 SENATOR He was said
To have been killed by footpads.
OEDIPUS So I heard;
But he who saw it is himself unseen.
1 SENATOR Well, if his bosom holds a grain of fear,
Curses like yours he never will abide!
OEDIPUS Whom the doing awes not, speaking cannot scare.
1 SENATOR Then there is one to expose him: here they come,
Bringing the godlike seer, the only man
Who has in him the tongue that cannot lie.

Enter TIRESIAS, *led by a boy.*

OEDIPUS Tiresias, thou who searchest everything,
Communicable or nameless, both in heaven
And on the earth—thou canst not see the city,
But knowest no less what pestilence visits it,
Wherefrom our only saviour and defence

We find, sir king, in thee. For Phoebus—if
Thou dost not know it from the messengers—
To us, who sent to ask him, sent word back,
That from this sickness no release should come,
Till we had found and slain the men who slew
Laius, or driven them, banished, from the land.
Wherefore do thou—not sparing augury,
Either through birds, or any other way
Thou hast of divination—save thyself,
And save the city, and me; save the whole mass
By this dead corpse infected; for in thee
Stands our existence; and for men, to help
With might and main is of all tasks the highest.

TIRESIAS Alas! How terrible it is to know,
Where no good comes of knowing! Of these matters
I was full well aware, but let them slip me;
Else I had not come hither.

OEDIPUS But what is it?
How out of heart thou hast come!

TIRESIAS Let me go home;
So shalt thou bear thy load most easily—
If thou wilt take my counsel—and I mine.

OEDIPUS Thou hast not spoken loyally, nor friendly
Toward the State that bred thee, cheating her
Of this response!

TIRESIAS Because I do not see
Thy words, not even thine, going to the mark;
So, not to be in the same plight—

1 SENATOR For Heaven's sake,
If thou hast knowledge, do not turn away,
When all of us implore thee suppliant!

TIRESIAS Ye
Are all unknowing; my say, in any sort,
I will not say, lest I display thy sorrow.

OEDIPUS What, you do know, and will not speak? Your mind
Is to betray us, and destroy the city?

TIRESIAS I will not bring remorse upon myself
And upon you. Why do you search these matters?
Vain, vain! I will not tell you.

OEDIPUS Worst of traitors!
For you would rouse a very stone to wrath—
Will you not speak out ever, but stand thus
Relentless and persistent?

TIRESIAS My offence
You censure; but your own, at home, you see not,
And yet blame me!

OEDIPUS Who would not take offence,
Hearing the words in which you flout the city?

TIRESIAS Well, it will come, keep silence as I may.

OEDIPUS And what will come should I not hear from you?

TIRESIAS I will declare no further. Storm at this,
If't please you, to the wildest height of anger!

OEDIPUS At least I will not, being so far in anger,
Spare anything of what is clear to me:
Know, I suspect you joined to hatch the deed;
Yea, did it—all but slaying with your own hands;
And if you were not blind, I should aver
The act was your work only!

TIRESIAS Was it so?
I charge you to abide by your decree
As you proclaimed it; nor from this day forth
Speak word to these, or me; being of this land
Yourself the abominable contaminator!

OEDIPUS So shamelessly set you this story on foot,
And think, perhaps, you shall go free?

TIRESIAS I am
Free! for I have in me the strength of truth.

OEDIPUS Who prompted you? for from your art it was not!

TIRESIAS Yourself! You made me speak, against my will.

OEDIPUS Speak! What? Repeat, that I may learn it better!

TIRESIAS Did you not understand me at first hearing,
Or are you tempting me, when you say "Speak!"

OEDIPUS Not so to say for certain; speak again.
TIRESIAS I say that you are Laius' murderer—
He whom you seek.
OEDIPUS Not without chastisement
Shall you, twice over, utter wounds!
TIRESIAS Then shall I
Say something more, that may incense you further?
OEDIPUS Say what you please; it will be said in vain.
TIRESIAS I say you know not in what worst of shame
You live together with those nearest you,
And see not in what evil plight you stand.
OEDIPUS Do you expect to go on revelling
In utterances like this?
TIRESIAS Yes, if the truth
Has any force at all.
OEDIPUS Why so it has,
Except for you; it is not so with you;
Blind as you are in eyes, and ears, and mind!
TIRESIAS Fool, you reproach me as not one of these
Shall not reproach you, soon!
OEDIPUS You cannot hurt me,
Nor any other who beholds the light,
Your life being all one night.
TIRESIAS Nor is it fated
You by my hand should fall; Apollo is
Sufficient; he will bring it all to pass.
OEDIPUS Are these inventions Creon's work, or yours?
TIRESIAS Your bane is no-ways Creon, but your own self.
OEDIPUS O riches, and dominion, and the craft
That excels craft, and makes life enviable,
How vast the grudge that is nursed up for you,
When for this sovereignty, which the state
Committed to my hands, unsought-for, free,
Creon, the trusty, the familiar friend,
With secret mines covets to oust me from it,
And has suborned a sorcerer like this,

An engine-botching crafty cogging knave,
Who has no eyes to see with, but for gain,
And was born blind in the art! Why, tell me now,
How stand your claims to prescience? How came it,
When the oracular monster was alive,
You said no word to set this people free?
And yet it was not for the first that came
To solve her riddle; sooth was needed then,
Which you could not afford; neither from birds,
Nor any inspiration; till I came,
The unlettered Oedipus, and ended her,
By sleight of wit, untaught of augury—
I whom you now seek to cast out, in hope
To stand upon the steps of Creon's throne!
You and the framer of this plot methinks
Shall rue your purge for guilt! Dotard you seem,
Else by experience you had come to know
What thoughts these are you think!

1 SENATOR As we conceive,
His words appear (and, Oedipus, your own,)
To have been said in anger; now not such
Our need, but rather to consider this—
How best to interpret the God's oracle.

TIRESIAS King as you are, we must be peers at least
In argument; I am your equal, there;
For I am Loxias'* servant, and not yours;
So never need be writ of Creon's train.
And since you have reproached me with my blindness,
I say—you have your sight, and do not see
What evils are about you, nor with whom,
Nor in what home you are dwelling. Do you know
From whom you are? Yea, you are ignorant
That to your own you are an enemy,
Whether on earth, alive, or under it.

* Apollo's.

Soon from this land shall drive you, stalking grim,
Your mother's and your father's two-edged curse,
With eyes then dark, though they look proudly now.
What place on earth shall not be harbour, then,
For your lamenting? What Cithaeron-peak*
Shall not be resonant soon, when you discern
What hymen-song was that, which wafted you
On a fair voyage, to foul anchorage
Under yon roof? and multitudes besides
Of ills you know not of shall level you
Down to your self—down to your children! Go,
Trample on Creon, and on this mouth of mine;
But know, there is not one of all mankind
That shall be bruised more utterly than you.

OEDIPUS Must I endure to hear all this from him?
Hence, to perdition! quickly hence! begone
Back from these walls, and turn you home again.

TIRESIAS But that you called me, I had not come hither.

OEDIPUS I did not know that you would utter folly;
Else I had scarce sent for you, to my house.

TIRESIAS Yea, such is what we seem, foolish to you,
And to your fathers, who begat you, wise.

OEDIPUS What fathers? Stop! Who was it gave me being?

TIRESIAS This day shall give you birth and death in one.

OEDIPUS How all too full of riddles and obscure
Is your discourse!

TIRESIAS Were you not excellent
At solving riddles?

OEDIPUS Ay, cast in my teeth
Matters in which you must allow my greatness!

TIRESIAS And yet this very fortune was your ruin!

OEDIPUS Well, if I saved this city, I care not.

TIRESIAS Well,
I am going; and you, boy, take me home.

* Mountain associated with many myths; see also page 37.

OEDIPUS Ay, let him.

Your turbulence impedes us, while you stay;
When you are gone, you can annoy no more.

[*Retires.*

TIRESIAS I go, having said that I came to say;
Not that I fear your frown; for you possess
No power to kill me; but I say to you—
The man you have been seeking, threatening him,
And loud proclaiming him for Laius' murder,
That man is here; believed a foreigner
Here sojourning; but shall be recognized
For Theban born hereafter; yet not pleased
In the event; for blind instead of seeing,
And poor for wealthy, to a foreign land,
A staff to point his footsteps, he shall go.
Also to his own sons he shall be found
Related as a brother, though their sire,
And of the woman from whose womb he came
Both son and spouse; one that has raised up seed
To his own father, and has murdered him.
Now get you in, and ponder what I say;
And if you can detect me in a lie,
Then come and say that I am no true seer.

[*Exeunt* TIRESIAS *and Boy.*

Chorus.

I. 1.

Who is he, who was said
By the Delphian soothsaying rock
To have wrought with hands blood-red
Nameless unspeakable deeds?
Time it were that he fled
Faster than storm-swift steeds!
For upon him springs with a shock,
Armed in thunder and fire,

The Child of Jove, at the head
Of the Destinies dread,
That follow, and will not tire.

I. 2.

For a word but now blazed clear
From Parnassus' snow-covered mound,*
To hunt down the Unknown!
He, through the forest drear,
By rocks, by cavernous ways,
Stalks, like a bull that strays,
Heartsore, footsore, alone;
Flying from Earth's central seat,
Flying the oracular sound
That with swift wings' beat
For ever circles him round.

II. 1.

Of a truth dark thoughts, yea dark and fell,
The augur wise doth arouse in me,
Who neither assent, nor yet gainsay;
And what to affirm, I cannot tell;
But I flutter in hope, unapt to see
Things of to-morrow, or to-day.

Why in Polybus' son** they should find a foe,
Or he in the heirs of Labdacus,
I know no cause, or of old, or late,
In test whereof I am now to go
Against the repute of Oedipus,
To avenge a Labdakid's unknown fate.

* Mount Parnassus is also associated with Apollo.
** Oedipus.

II. 2.

True, Zeus indeed, and Apollo, are wise,
And knowers of what concerns mankind;
But that word of a seer, a man like me,
Weighs more than mine, for a man to prize,
Is all unsure. Yea, one man's mind
May surpass another's in subtlety;

But never will I, till I see the rest,
Assent to those who accuse him now.
I saw how the air-borne Maiden came
Against him, and proved him wise, by the test,
And good to the state; and for this, I trow,
He shall not, ever, be put to shame.

Enter CREON.

CREON I am come hither, fellow citizens,
Having been told that Oedipus the king
Lays grievous accusations to my charge,
Which I will not endure. For if he fancies
He in our present troubles has endured
Aught at my hands, either in word or deed,
Tending to harm him, I have no desire
My life should be prolonged, bearing this blame.
The injury that such a word may do
Is no mere trifle, but more vast than any,
If I am to be called a criminal
Here in the town, and by my friends, and you.

1 SENATOR Nay, the reproach, it may be, rather came
Through stress of anger, than advisedly.

CREON But it was plainly said, by my advice
The prophet gave false answers.

1 SENATOR It was said;
But how advised I know not.

CREON Was this charge

Of a set mind, and with set countenance
Imputed against me?

1 SENATOR I do not know.
I have no eyes for what my masters do.
But here he comes, himself, forth of the palace.

Enter OEDIPUS.

OEDIPUS Fellow, how cam'st thou hither? Dost thou boast
So great a front of daring, as to come
Under my roof, the assassin clear of me,
And manifest pirate of my royalty?
Tell me, by heaven, did you detect in me
The bearing of a craven, or a fool,
That you laid plans to do it; or suppose
I should not recognize your work in this,
Creeping on slily, and defend myself?
Is it not folly, this attempt of yours,
Without a following, without friends, to hunt
After a throne, a thing which is achieved
By aid of followers and much revenue?

CREON Do me this favour; hear me say as much
As you have said; and then, yourself decide.

OEDIPUS You are quick to talk, but I am slow to learn
Of you; for I have found you contrary
And dangerous to me.

CREON Now, this same thing
First hear, how I shall state it.

OEDIPUS This same thing
Do not tell me—that you are not a villain!

CREON If you suppose your arrogance weighs aught
Apart from reason, you are much astray.

OEDIPUS If you suppose you can escape the pain
Due for a kinsman's wrong, you are astray!

CREON You speak with justice; I agree! But tell me,
How is it that you say I injured you?

OEDIPUS Did you persuade me that I ought to send
To fetch that canting soothsayer, or no?

CREON Why yes, and now, I am of the same mind, still.
OEDIPUS How long is it since Laius—
CREON What? I know not.
OEDIPUS Died—disappeared, murdered by violence?
CREON Long seasons might be numbered, long gone by.
OEDIPUS Well, did this seer then practise in the craft?
CREON Yes, just as wise, and just as much revered.
OEDIPUS And did he at that time say one word of me?
CREON Well, nowhere in my presence, anyhow.
OEDIPUS But did not you hold inquest for the dead?
CREON We did, of course; and got no evidence.
OEDIPUS Well then, how came it that this wiseacre
Did not say these things then?
CREON I do not know.
In matters where I have no cognizance
I hold my tongue.
OEDIPUS This much, at least, you know,
And if you are wise, will say!
CREON And what is that?
For if I know it, I shall not refuse.
OEDIPUS Why, that unless he had conspired with you
He never would have said that Laius' murder
Was of my doing!
CREON If he says so, you know.
Only I claim to know that first from you,
Which you put now to me.
OEDIPUS Learn anything!
For I shall not be found a murderer.
CREON Well then; you have my sister to your wife?
OEDIPUS There's no denying that question.
CREON And with her
Rule equal, and in common hold the land?
OEDIPUS All she may wish for she obtains of me.
CREON And make I not a third, equal with you?
OEDIPUS Ay, there appears your friendship's falsity.
CREON Not if you reason with yourself, as I.
And note this first; if you can think that any

Would rather choose a sovereignty, with fears,
Than the same power, with undisturbed repose?
Neither am I, by nature, covetous
To be a king, rather than play the king,
Nor any man who has sagacity.
Now I have all things, without fear, from you;
Reigned I myself, I must do much I hated.
How were a throne, then, pleasanter for me
Than painless empire and authority?
I am not yet so blinded as to wish
For honour, other than is joined with gain.
Now am I hail-fellow-well-met with all;
Now every man gives me good-morrow; now
The waiters on your favour fawn on me;
For all their prospering depends thereby.
Then how should I exchange this lot for yours?
A mind well balanced cannot turn to crime.
I neither am in love with this design,
Nor, in a comrade, would I suffer it.
For proof of which, first, go to Pytho; ask
For the oracles, if I declared them truly;
Next, if you can detect me in the act
Of any conjuration with the seer,
Then, by a double vote, not one alone,
Mine and your own, take me, and take my life;
But do not, on a dubious argument,
Charge me beside the facts. For just it is not,
To hold bad men for good, good men for bad,
To no good end; nay, 'twere all one to me
To throw away a friend, a worthy one,
And one's own life, which most of all one values.
Ah well; in time, you will see these things plainly;
For time alone shews a man's honesty,
But in one day you may discern his guilt.

1 SENATOR His words sound fair—to one who fears to fall;
For swift in counsel is unsafe, my liege.

OEDIPUS When he who plots against me in the dark

Comes swiftly on, I must be swift in turn.
If I stay quiet, his ends will have been gained,
And mine all missed.

CREON What is it that you want?
To expel me from the country?

OEDIPUS Not at all.
Your death I purpose, not your banishment.

CREON Not without shewing, first, what a thing is jealousy!

OEDIPUS You talk like one who will not yield, nor heed.

CREON Because I see you mean injuriously.

OEDIPUS Not to myself!

CREON No more you ought to me!

OEDIPUS You are a traitor!

CREON What if you are no judge?

OEDIPUS I must be ruler.

CREON Not if you rule badly.

OEDIPUS City, my city!

CREON The city is mine too,
And not yours only.

1 SENATOR Good my lords, have done,
Here is Jocasta; in good time, I see her
Come to you from the palace; with her aid
'Twere meet to appease your present difference.

Enter JOCASTA.

JOCASTA Unhappy men, what was it made you raise
This senseless broil of words? Are you not both
Ashamed of stirring private grievances,
The land being thus afflicted? Get you in—
And, Creon, do you go home; push not mere nothing
On to some terrible calamity!

CREON Sister, your husband Oedipus thinks fit
To treat me villainously; choosing for me
Of two bad things, one; to expatriate me,
Or seize and kill me.

OEDIPUS I admit it, wife;

not naming her

For I have found him out in an offence
Against my person, joined with treachery.

CREON So may I never thrive, but perish, banned
Of Heaven, if I have done a thing to you
Of what you charge against me!

JOCASTA Oedipus!
O in Heaven's name believe it! Above all
Revere this oath in heaven; secondly
Myself, and these, who stand before you here.

1 SENATOR Hear her, my king! With wisdom and goodwill
I pray you hear!

OEDIPUS What would you have me grant?

1 SENATOR Respect his word; no bauble, heretofore;
And by this oath made weighty.

OEDIPUS Do you know
For what you ask?

1 SENATOR I do.

OEDIPUS Say what you mean, then!

1 SENATOR That you expel not, ever, with disgrace,
The friend, who has abjured it, on a charge
Void of clear proof.

OEDIPUS Now, understand it well;
Seek this, you seek my death or exile!

1 SENATOR Nay,
By the Sun-god, first of all Gods in heaven!
So may I perish, to the uttermost,
Cut off from Heaven, without the help of men,
If I have such a thought! But the land's waste
Will break my heart with grief—and that this woe,
Your strife, is added to its former woe.

OEDIPUS Well, let him go, though I get slain outright,
Or thrust by force, dishonoured, from the land;
Your voice, not his, makes me compassionate,
Pleading for pity; he, where'er he be,
Shall have my hatred.

CREON You display your spleen

In yielding; but, when your wrath passes bound,
Are formidable! Tempers such as yours
Most grievous are to their own selves to bear,
Not without justice.

OEDIPUS Leave me; get you gone!

CREON I go; you know me not; these know me honest.

[*Exit.*

1 SENATOR Lady, what hinders you from taking him
Into the house?

JOCASTA I would know how this happened.

1 SENATOR A blind surmise arose, out of mere babble;
But even what is unjust inflicts a sting.

JOCASTA On part of both?

1 SENATOR Yes truly.

JOCASTA And what was said?

1 SENATOR Enough it seems, enough it seems to me,
Under the former trouble of the land,
To leave this where it lies.

OEDIPUS Do you perceive
How far you are carried—a well-meaning man!
Slurring my anger thus, and blunting it?

1 SENATOR I said it, O my king, not once alone—
But be assured, I should have shewn myself
Robbed of my wits, useless for work of wit,
Renouncing thee! who didst impel the sails
Of my dear land, baffled mid straits, right onward,
And it may be, wilt waft her safely now!

JOCASTA For Heaven's sake tell me too, my lord, what was it
Caused you so deep an anger?

OEDIPUS I will tell you;
For I respect you, lady, more than these;
'Twas Creon—at plots which he has laid for me.

JOCASTA If you will charge the quarrel in plain terms,
Why speak!

OEDIPUS He says that I am Laius' slayer.

JOCASTA Of his own knowledge, or on hearsay?

OEDIPUS Nay,
But by citation of a knavish seer;
As for himself, he keeps his words blame-free.

JOCASTA Now set you free from thought of that you talk of;
Listen and learn, nothing in human life
Turns on the soothsayer's art. Tokens of this
I'll show you in few words. To Laius once
There came an oracle, I do not say
From Phoebus' self, but from his ministers,
That so it should befall, that he should die
By a son's hands, whom he should have by me.
And him—the story goes—robbers abroad
Have murdered, at a place where three roads meet;
While from our son's birth not three days went by
Before, with ankles pinned, he cast him out,
By hands of others, on a pathless moor.
And so Apollo did not bring about
That he should be his father's murderer;
Nor yet that Laius should endure the stroke
At his son's hands, of which he was afraid.
This is what came of soothsayers' oracles;
Whereof take thou no heed. That which we lack,
If a God seek, himself will soon reveal.

OEDIPUS What perturbation and perplexity
Take hold upon me, woman, hearing you!

JOCASTA What stress of trouble is on you, that you say so?

OEDIPUS I thought I heard you say Laius was slain
Where three roads meet!

JOCASTA Yes, so the rumour ran,
And so runs still.

OEDIPUS And where might be the spot
Where this befell?

JOCASTA Phocis the land is named;
There are two separate roads converge in one
From Daulia and Delphi.

OEDIPUS And what time
Has passed since then?

JOCASTA It was but just before
You were installed as ruler of the land,
The tidings reached the city.

OEDIPUS God of Heaven!
What would'st thou do unto me!

JOCASTA Oedipus,
What is it on your mind?

OEDIPUS Ask me not yet.
But Laius—say, what was he like? what prime
Of youth had he attained to?

JOCASTA He was tall;
The first white flowers had blossomed in his hair;
His figure was not much unlike your own.

OEDIPUS Me miserable! It seems I have but now
Proffered myself to a tremendous curse
Not knowing!

JOCASTA How say you? I tremble, O my lord,
To gaze upon you!

OEDIPUS I am sore afraid
The prophet was not blind; but you will make
More certain, if you answer one thing more.

JOCASTA Indeed I tremble; but the thing you ask
I'll answer, when I know it.

OEDIPUS Was he going
Poorly attended, or with many spears
About him, like a prince?

JOCASTA But five in all;
One was a herald; and one carriage held
Laius himself,

OEDIPUS O, it is plain already!
Woman, who was it told this tale to you?

JOCASTA A servant, who alone came safe away.

OEDIPUS Is he perchance now present, in the house?

JOCASTA Why no; for after he was come from thence,
And saw you governing, and Laius dead,
He came and touched my hand, and begged of me
To send him to the fields and sheep-meadows,

So he might be as far as possible
From eyesight of the townsmen; and I sent him;
For he was worthy, for a slave, to obtain
Even greater favours.

OEDIPUS Could we have him back
Quickly?

JOCASTA We could. But why this order?

OEDIPUS Wife,
I fear me I have spoken far too much;
Wherefore I wish to see him.

JOCASTA He shall come!
But I am worthy, in my turn, to know
What weighs so heavily upon you, Sir?

OEDIPUS And you shall know; since I have passed so far
The bounds of apprehension. For to whom
Could I impart, passing through such a need,
Greater in place—if that were all—than you?
—I am the son of Polybus of Corinth,
And of a Dorian mother, Merope.
And I was counted most preëminent
Among the townsmen there; up to the time
A circumstance befell me, of this fashion—
Worthy of wonder, though of my concern
Unworthy. At the board a drunken fellow
Over his cups called me a changeling;
And I, being indignant—all that day
Hardly refrained—but on the morrow went
And taxed my parents with it to their face;
Who took the scandal grievously, of him
Who launched the story. Well, with what they said
I was content; and yet the thing still galled me;
For it spread far. So without cognizance
Of sire or mother I set out to go
To Pytho.* Phoebus sent me of my quest

* The Pythian oracle at Delphi, as on page 3.

Bootless away; but other terrible
And strange and lamentable things revealed,
Saying I should wed my mother, and produce
A race intolerable for men to see,
And be my natural father's murderer.
When I heard that, measuring where Corinth stands
Even thereafter by the stars alone,
Where I might never think to see fulfilled
The scandals of ill prophecies of me,
I fled, an exile. As I journeyed on,
I found myself upon the self-same spot
Where, you say, this king perished. In your ears,
Wife, I will tell the whole. When in my travels
I was come near this place where three roads meet,
There met me a herald, and a man that rode
In a colt-carriage, as you tell of him,
And from the track the leader, by main force,
And the old man himself, would thrust me. I,
Being enraged, strike him who jostled me—
The driver—and the old man, when he saw it,
Watching as I was passing, from the car
With his goad's fork smote me upon the head.
He paid, though! duly I say not; but in brief,
Smitten by the staff in this right hand of mine,
Out of the middle of the carriage straight
He rolls down headlong; and I slay them all!
But if there be a semblance to connect
This nameless man with Laius, who is now
More miserable than I am? Who on earth
Could have been born with more of hate from heaven?
Whom never citizen or stranger may
Receive into their dwellings, or accost,
But must thrust out of doors; and 'tis no other
Laid all these curses on myself, than I!
Yea, with embraces of the arms whereby
He perished, I pollute my victim's bed!

Am I not vile? Am I not all unclean?
If I must fly, and flying, never can
See my own folk, or on my native land
Set foot, or else must with my mother wed,
And slay my father Polybus, who begat
And bred me? Would he not speak truly of me
Who judged these things sent by some barbarous Power?
Never, you sacred majesties of Heaven,
Never may I behold that day; but pass
Out of men's sight, ere I shall see myself
Touched by the stain of such a destiny!

1 SENATOR My liege, these things affect us grievously;
Still, till you hear his story who was by,
Do not lose hope!

OEDIPUS Yea, so much hope is left,
Merely to wait for him, the herdsman.

JOCASTA Well,
Suppose him here, what do you want of him?

OEDIPUS I'll tell you; if he should be found to say
Just what you said, I shall be clear from harm.

JOCASTA What did you hear me say, that did not tally?

OEDIPUS You were just telling me that he made mention
Of "robbers"—"men"—as Laius' murderers.
Now if he shall affirm their number still,
I did not slay him. One cannot be the same
As many. But if he shall speak of one—
One only, it is evident this deed
Already will have been brought home to me.

JOCASTA But be assured, that was the word, quite plainly!
And now he cannot blot it out again.
Not I alone, but the whole city heard it.
Then, even if he shift from his first tale,
Not so, my lord, will he at all explain
The death of Laius, as it should have been,
Whom Loxias declared my son must slay!
And after all, the poor thing never killed him,

But died itself before! so that henceforth
I do not mean to look to left or right
For fear of soothsaying!

OEDIPUS You are well advised.
Still, send and fetch the labourer; do not miss it.

JOCASTA I will send quickly. Now let us go within.
I would do nothing that displeases you.

[*Exeunt* OEDIPUS *and* JOCASTA.

Chorus.

I. 1.

Let it be mine to keep
The holy purity of word and deed
Foreguided all by mandates from on high
Born in the ethereal region of the sky,
Their only sire Olympus; them nor seed
Of mortal man brought forth, nor Lethe cold
Shall ever lay to sleep;
In them Deity is great, and grows not old.

I. 2.

Pride is the germ of kings;
Pride, when puffed up, vainly, with many things
Unseasonable, unfitting, mounts the wall,
Only to hurry to that fatal fall,
Where feet are vain to serve her. But the task
Propitious to the city GOD I ask
Never to take away!
GOD I will never cease to hold my stay.

II. 1.

But if any man proceed
Insolently in word or deed,
Without fear of right, or care

For the seats where Virtues are,
Him, for his ill-omened pride,
Let an evil death betide!
If honestly his gear he will not gain,
Nor keep himself from deeds unholy,
Nor from inviolable things abstain,
Blinded by folly.
In such a course, what mortal from his heart
Dart upon dart
Can hope to avert of indignation?
Yea, and if acts like these are held in estimation,
Why dance we here our part?

II. 2.

Never to the inviolate hearth
At the navel of the earth,*
Nor to Abae's fane, in prayer,
Nor the Olympian, will I fare,
If it shall not so befall
Manifestly unto all.
But O our king—if thou art named aright—
Zeus, that art Lord of all things ever,
Be this not hid from Thee, nor from Thy might
Which endeth never.
For now already men invalidate
The dooms of Fate
Uttered for Laius, fading slowly;
Apollo's name and rites are nowhere now kept holy;
Worship is out of date.

Enter JOCASTA, *attended.*

JOCASTA Lords of the land, it came into my heart
To approach the temples of the Deities,
Taking in hand these garlands, and this incense;

* The oracle at Delphi.

For Oedipus lets his mind float too light
Upon the eddies of all kinds of grief;
Nor will he, like a man of soberness,
Measure the new by knowledge of the old,
But is at mercy of whoever speaks,
If he but speak the language of despair.
I can do nothing by exhorting him.
Wherefore, Lycean Phoebus, unto thee—
For thou art very near us—I am come.
Bringing these offerings, a petitioner
That thou afford us fair deliverance;
Since now we are all frighted, seeing him—
The vessel's pilot, as 'twere—panic-stricken.

Enter a Messenger.

MESSENGER Sirs, might I learn of you, where is the palace
Of Oedipus the King? or rather, where
He is himself, if you know, tell me.
1 SENATOR Stranger,
This is his dwelling, and he is within;
This lady is his children's mother, too.
MESSENGER A blessing ever be on hers and her,
Who is, in such a perfect sort, his wife!
JOCASTA The like be with you too, as you deserve,
Sir, for your compliment. But say what end
You come for, and what news you wish to tell.
MESSENGER Good to the house, and to your husband, lady.
JOCASTA Of what sort? and from whom come you?
MESSENGER From Corinth.
In that which I am now about to say
May you find pleasure! and why not? And yet
Perhaps you may be sorry.
JOCASTA But what is it?
How can it carry such ambiguous force?
MESSENGER The dwellers in the land of Isthmia,
As was there said, intend to appoint him king.

JOCASTA What! Is not Polybus, the old prince, still reigning?
MESSENGER No, truly; he is Death's subject, in the grave.
JOCASTA How say you, father? Is Polybus no more?
MESSENGER I stake my life upon it, if I lie!
JOCASTA Run, girl, and tell your master instantly.
[*Exit an attendant.*
O prophecies of Gods, where are you now!
Oedipus fled, long since, from this man's presence,
Fearing to kill him; and now he has died
A natural death, not by his means at all!

Enter OEDIPUS.

OEDIPUS O my most dear Jocasta, wife of mine,
Why did you fetch me hither from the house?
JOCASTA Hear this man speak! Listen and mark, to what
The dark responses of the God are come!
OEDIPUS And who is this? What says he?
JOCASTA He's from Corinth,
To tell us that your father Polybus
Lives no more, but is dead!
OEDIPUS What say you, sir?
Tell your own tale yourself.
MESSENGER If first of all
I must deliver this for certainty,
Know well, that he has gone the way of mortals.
OEDIPUS Was it by treason, or some chance disease?
MESSENGER A little shock prostrates an aged frame!
OEDIPUS Sickness, you mean, was my poor father's end?
MESSENGER Yes, and old age; his term of life was full.
OEDIPUS Heigh ho! Why, wife! why should a man regard
The oracular hearth of Pytho, or the birds
Cawing above us, by whose canons I
Was to have slain my father? He is dead,
And buried out of sight; and here am I,
Laying no finger to the instrument,
(Unless, indeed, he pined for want of me,

And so, I killed him!) Well, Polybus is gone;
And with him all those oracles of ours
Bundled to Hades, for old songs, together!

JOCASTA Did I not say so all along?

OEDIPUS You did;
But I was led astray by fear.

JOCASTA Well, now
Let none of these predictions any more
Weigh on your mind!

OEDIPUS And how can I help dreading
My mother's bed?

JOCASTA But why should men be fearful,
O'er whom Fortune is mistress, and foreknowledge
Of nothing sure? Best take life easily,
As a man may. For that maternal wedding,
Have you no fear; for many men ere now
Have dreamed as much; but he who by such dreams
Sets nothing, has the easiest life of it.

OEDIPUS All these things would have been well said of you,
Were not my mother living still; but now,
She being alive, there is all need of dread;
Though you say well.

JOCASTA And yet your father's burial
Lets in much daylight!

OEDIPUS I acknowledge, much.
Still, her who lives I fear.

MESSENGER But at what woman
Are you dismayed?

OEDIPUS At Merope, old man,
The wife of Polybus.

MESSENGER And what of her
Causes you terror?

OEDIPUS A dark oracle,
Stranger, from heaven.

MESSENGER May it be put in words?
Or is it wrong another man should know it?

OEDIPUS No, not at all. Why, Loxias declared
That I should one day marry my own mother,
And with my own hands shed my father's blood.
Wherefore from Corinth I have kept away
Far, for long years; and prospered; none the less
It is most sweet to see one's parents' face.

MESSENGER And in this apprehension you became
An emigrant from Corinth?

OEDIPUS And, old man,
Desiring not to be a parricide.

MESSENGER Why should I not deliver you, my liege—
Since my intent in coming here was good—
Out of this fear?

OEDIPUS Indeed you would obtain
Good guerdon from me.

MESSENGER And indeed for this
Chiefest I came, that upon your return
I might in some sort benefit.

OEDIPUS But I
Will never go, to meet my parents there!

MESSENGER O son, 'tis plain you know not what you do!

OEDIPUS How so, old man? in Heaven's name tell me!

MESSENGER If
On this account you shun the journey home!

OEDIPUS Of course I fear lest Phoebus turn out true.

MESSENGER Lest through your parents you incur foul stain?

OEDIPUS Yes, father, yes; that is what always scares me.

MESSENGER Now do you know you tremble, really, at nothing?

OEDIPUS How can that be, if I was born their child?

MESSENGER Because Polybus was nought akin to you!

OEDIPUS What, did not Polybus beget me?

MESSENGER No,
No more than I did; just so much as I!

OEDIPUS How, my own sire no more than—nobody?

MESSENGER But neither he begat you, nor did I.

OEDIPUS Then from what motive did he call me son?

MESSENGER Look here; he had you as a gift from me.
OEDIPUS And loved me then, so much, at second hand?
MESSENGER Yes, his long childlessness prevailed on him.
OEDIPUS And did you find or purchase me, to give him?
MESSENGER I found you in Cithaeron's wooded dells.
OEDIPUS How came you to be journeying in these parts?
MESSENGER I tended flocks upon the mountains here.
OEDIPUS You were a shepherd, and you ranged for hire?
MESSENGER But at the same time your preserver, son!
OEDIPUS You found me in distress? What was my trouble?
MESSENGER Your ankle joints may witness.
OEDIPUS O, why speak you
Of that old evil?
MESSENGER I untied you, when
You had the soles of both your feet bored through.
OEDIPUS A shameful sort of swaddling bands were mine.
MESSENGER Such, that from them you had the name you bear.*
OEDIPUS Tell me, by heaven! at sire's or mother's hand—
MESSENGER I know not: he who gave you knows of that
Better than I.
OEDIPUS You got me from another?
You did not find me?
MESSENGER No, another shepherd
Gave you to me.
OEDIPUS Who was he? are you able
To point him out?
MESSENGER They said that he was one
Of those who followed Laius, whom you know.
OEDIPUS Him who was once the monarch of this land?
MESSENGER Precisely! This man was his herdsman.
OEDIPUS Now
Is this man still alive for me to see?
MESSENGER You must know best, the people of the place.
OEDIPUS Is any here among you bystanders,

* By a folk etymology, the name Oedipus is taken to mean "swollen feet."

Who knows the herdsman whom he tells us of,
From seeing him, either in the fields or here?
Speak! it were time that this had been cleared up.

1 SENATOR I think he is no other than that peasant
Whom you were taking pains to find, before;
But she could say as well as any one—
Jocasta.

OEDIPUS Lady, you remember him
Whose coming we were wishing for but now;
Does he mean him?

JOCASTA Why ask who 'twas he spoke of?
Nay, never mind—never remember it—
'Twas idly spoken!

OEDIPUS Nay, it cannot be
That having such a clue I should refuse
To solve the mystery of my parentage!

JOCASTA For Heaven's sake, if you care for your own life,
Don't seek it! I am sick, and that's enough!

OEDIPUS Courage! At least, if I be thrice a slave,
Born so three-deep, it cannot injure you!

JOCASTA But I beseech you, hearken! Do not do it!

OEDIPUS I will not hearken—not to know the whole.

JOCASTA I mean well; and I tell you for the best!

OEDIPUS What you call best is an old sore of mine.

JOCASTA Wretch, what thou art O might'st thou never know!

OEDIPUS Will some one go and fetch the herdsman hither?
She is welcome to her gilded lineage!

JOCASTA O
Woe, woe, unhappy! This is all I have
To say to thee, and no word more, for ever!

[*Exit.*

1 SENATOR Why has the woman vanished, Oedipus,
Driven so wild with grief? I am afraid
Out of her silence will break forth some trouble.

OEDIPUS Break out what will, I shall not hesitate,
Low though it be, to trace the source of me.

But she, perhaps, being, as a woman, proud,
Of my unfit extraction is ashamed.
—I deem myself the child of Fortune! I
Shall not be shamed of her, who favours me;
Seeing I have her for mother; and for kin
The limitary Moons, that found me small,
That fashioned me for great! Parented thus,
How could I ever in the issue prove
Other—that I should leave my birth unknown?

Chorus

1.

If I am a true seer,
My mind from error clear,
Tomorrow's moon shall not pass over us,
Ere, O Cithaeron, we
Shall magnify in thee
The land, the lap, the womb of Oedipus;
And we shall hymn thy praises, for good things
Of thy bestowing, done unto our kings.
Yea, Phoebus, if thou wilt, amen, so might it be!

2.

Who bare thee? Which, O child,
Over the mountain-wild
Sought to by Pan of the immortal Maids?
Or Loxias—was he
The sire who fathered thee?
For dear to him are all the upland glades.
Was it Cyllene's lord* acquired a son,
Or Bacchus, dweller on the heights, from one
Of those he liefest loves, Oreads** of Helicon?

* Hermes.
** Mountain nymphs.

Enter Attendants with an Old Man, a Shepherd.

OEDIPUS If I may guess, who never met with him,
I think I see that herdsman, Senators,
We have long been seeking; for his ripe old age
Harmoniously accords with this man's measure;
Besides, I recognize the men who bring him
As of my household; but in certainty
You can perhaps exceed me, who beheld
The herdsman formerly.

1 SENATOR Why, to be sure,
I recognize him; for he was a man
Trusty as any Laius ever had
About his pastures.

OEDIPUS You I ask the first,
The Corinthian stranger; do you speak of him?

MESSENGER Yes, him you see.

OEDIPUS Sirrah, old man, look here;
Answer my questions. Were you Laius' man?

OLD MAN Truly his thrall; not bought, but bred at home.

OEDIPUS Minding what work, or in what character?

OLD MAN Most of my time I went after the flocks.

OEDIPUS In what directions, chiefly, were your folds?

OLD MAN There was Cithaeron; and a bit near by.

OEDIPUS Do you know this man, then? Did you see him there?

OLD MAN Him? After what? What man do you mean?

OEDIPUS This fellow
Here present; did you ever meet with him?

OLD MAN Not so to say off-hand, from memory.

MESSENGER And that's no wonder, sir; but beyond doubt
I will remind him, though he has forgotten,
I am quite sure he knows, once on a time,
When in the bit about Cithaeron there—
He with two flocks together, I with one—
I was his neighbour for three whole half years
From spring-tide onward to the Bear-ward's* day;

* The constellation Bootes.

And with the winter to my folds I drove,
And he to Laius' stables. Are these facts,
Or are they not—what I am saying?

OLD MAN Yes,
You speak the truth; but it was long ago.

MESSENGER Come, say now, don't you mind that you then gave me
A baby boy to bring up for my own?

OLD MAN What do you mean? Why do you ask it me?

MESSENGER This is the man, good fellow; who was then
A youngling!

OLD MAN Out upon you! Hold your peace!

OEDIPUS Nay, old man, do not chide him; for your words
Deserve a chiding rather than his own!

OLD MAN O best of masters, what is my offence?

OEDIPUS Not telling of that boy he asks about.

OLD MAN He says he knows not what! He is all astray!

OEDIPUS You will not speak of grace—you shall perforce!

OLD MAN Do not for God's sake harm me, an old man!

OEDIPUS Quick, some one, twist his hands behind him!

OLD MAN Wretch,
What have I done? What do you want to know?

OEDIPUS Did you give him that boy he asks about?

OLD MAN I gave it him. Would I had died that day!

OEDIPUS Tell the whole truth, or you will come to it!

OLD MAN I am undone far more, though, if I speak!

OEDIPUS The man is trifling with us, I believe.

OLD MAN No, no; I said I gave it, long ago!

OEDIPUS Where did you get it? At home, or from some other?

OLD MAN It was not mine; another gave it me.

OEDIPUS Which of these citizens? and from what roof?

OLD MAN Don't, master, for God's sake, don't ask me more!

OEDIPUS You are a dead man, if I speak again!

OLD MAN Then—'twas a child—of Laius' household.

OEDIPUS What,
Slave-born? or one of his own family?

OLD MAN O, I am at the horror, now, to speak!

OEDIPUS And I to hear. But I must hear—no less.

OLD MAN Truly it was called his son; but she within,
Your lady, could best tell you how it was.

OEDIPUS Did she then give it you?

OLD MAN My lord, even so.

OEDIPUS For what?

OLD MAN For me to make away with it.

OEDIPUS Herself the mother? miserable!

OLD MAN In dread
Of evil prophecies—

OEDIPUS What prophecies?

OLD MAN That he should kill his parents, it was said.

OEDIPUS How came you then to give it to this old man?

OLD MAN For pity, O my master! thinking he
Would carry it away to other soil,
From whence he came; but he to the worst of harms
Saved it! for if thou art the man he says,
Sure thou wast born destined to misery!

OEDIPUS Woe! woe! It is all plain, indeed! O Light,
This be the last time I shall gaze on thee,
Who am revealed to have been born of those
Of whom I ought not—to have wedded whom
I ought not—and slain whom I might not slay!

[*Exit.*

CLIMAX!

Chorus.

I. 1.

O generations of mankind!
How do I find
Your lives nought worth at all!
For who is he—what state
Is there, more fortunate
Than only to seem great,
And then, to fall?
I having thee for pattern, and thy lot—
Thine, O poor Oedipus—I envy not

Aught in mortality;
For this is he

I. 2.

Who, shooting far beyond the rest,
Won wealth all-blest,
Slaying, Zeus, thy monster-maid,
Crook-taloned, boding; and
Who did arise and stand
Betwixt death and our land,
A tower of aid;
Yea for this cause thou hast been named our king,
And honoured in the highest, governing
The city of Thebae great
In royal state.

II. 1.

And now, who lives more utterly undone?
Who with sad woes, who with mischances rude
Stands closer yoked by life's vicissitude?
O honoured head of Oedipus, for whom
Within the same wide haven there was room
To come—child, to the birth—
Sire, to the nuptial bower,
How could the furrows of thy parent earth—
How could they suffer thee, O hapless one,
In silence, to this hour?

II. 2.

Time found thee out—Time who sees everything—
Unwittingly guilty; and arraigns thee now
Consort ill-sorted, unto whom are bred
Sons of thy getting, in thine own birth-bed.
O scion of Laius' race,

Would I had never never seen thy face!
For I lament, even as from lips that sing
Pouring a dirge; yet verily it was thou
Gav'st me to rise
And breathe again, and close my watching eyes.

Enter a second MESSENGER.

2 MESSENGER O you most honoured ever of this land,
What deeds have you to hear, what sights to see,
What sorrow to endure, if you still cherish
The house of Labdacus with loyalty?
For Ister* I suppose or Phasis'** wave
Never could purge this dwelling from the ills
It covers—or shall instantly reveal,
Invited, not inflicted; of all wounds,
Those that seem wilful are the worst to bear.

1 SENATOR There was no lack, in what we knew before,
Of lamentable; what have you more to say?

2 MESSENGER The speediest of all tales to hear and tell;
The illustrious Jocasta is no more.

1 SENATOR Unhappy woman! From what cause?

2 MESSENGER Self-slain.
Of what befell the saddest part is spared;
For you were not a witness. None the less
So far as I can tell it you shall hear
Her miserable story. When she passed
So frantically inside the vestibule,
She went straight onward to the bed-chamber,
With both her hands tearing her hair; the doors
She dashed to as she entered, crying out
On Laius, long since dead, calling to mind
His fore-begotten offspring, by whose hands
He, she said, died, and left to his own seed

* The Danube.
** A river emptying into the Black Sea.

Its mother's most unnatural bearing-bed.
Nor did she not bewail that nuptial-couch
Where she brought forth, unhappy, brood on brood,
Spouse to her spouse, and children to her child.
And then—I know no further how she perished;
For Oedipus brake in, crying aloud;
For whom it was impossible to watch
The ending of her misery; but on him
We gazed, as he went raging all about,
Beseeching us to furnish him a sword
And say where he could find his wife—no wife,
Rather the mother-soil both of himself
And children; and, as he raved thus, some Power
Shews him—at least, none of us present did.
Then, shouting loud, he sprang upon the doors
As following some guide, and burst the bars
Out of their sockets, and alights within.
There we beheld his wife hanging, entwined
In a twined noose. He seeing her, with a groan
Looses the halter; then, when on the ground
Lay the poor wretch, dreadful it was to see
What followed; snatching from her dress gold pins
Wherewith she was adorned, he lifted them,
And smote the nerves of his own eyeballs, saying
Something like this—that they should see no more
Evils like those he had endured or wrought;
Darkling, thereafter, let them gaze on forms
He might not see, and fail to recognize
The faces he desired! Chanting this burden,
Not once, but many times, he raised his hand
And stabbed his eyes; so that from both of them
The blood ran down his face, not drop by drop,
But all at once, in a dark shower of gore.
—These are the ills that from a two-fold source,
Not one alone, but in both wife and spouse,
Mingled together, have burst forth at once.

Their former pristine happiness indeed
Was happiness before; but in this hour
Shame—lamentation—Atè*—death—of all
That has a name of evil, nought's away!

1 SENATOR And does he stand in any respite now
Of misery, poor soul?

2 MESSENGER He calls aloud
For some one to undo the bolts, and shew
To all the Cadmeans him, his father's slayer—
His mother's—uttering words unhallowed—words
I may not speak; that he will cast himself
Forth of the land, abide no more at home
Under the curse of his own cursing. Nay,
But he lacks force, and guidance; for his sickness
Is more than man can bear. See for yourself;
For these gates open, and you will straight behold
A sight—such as even he that loathes must pity!

Enter OEDIPUS *blind.*

Chorus.

O sorrow, lamentable for eyes to see!
Sorest of all past ills encountering me!
What frenzy, O wretch, is this, that came on thee?

What Deity was it that with a leap so great—
Farther than farthest—sprang on thy sad fate?
Woe is me, woe is me for thee—unfortunate!

Fain would I gaze at thee, would ask thee much,
Many things learn of thee, wert thou not such
As I may not even behold, as I shudder to touch.

OEDIPUS Me miserable! Whither must I go?
Ah whither flits my voice, borne to and fro?
Thou Power unseen, how hast thou brought me low!

* Doom caused by guilt and ignorance.

1 SENATOR To ills, intolerable to hear or see.

OEDIPUS Thou horror of thick darkness overspread,
Thou shadow of unutterable dread
Not to be stemmed or stayed, fallen on my head—

Woe's me once more! How crowd upon my heart
Stings of these wounds, and memories of woe!

1 SENATOR No marvel if thou bear a double smart
And writhe, so stricken, with a two-fold throe!

OEDIPUS Still art thou near me—ready still to tend
And to endure me, faithful to the end,
Blind as I am, with kindness, O my friend!

For strange thou art not; but full well I know
That voice of thine, all darkling though I be.

1 SENATOR Rash man, how could'st thou bear to outrage so
Thine eyes? What Power was it, that wrought on thee?

OEDIPUS Apollo, Apollo fulfils,
O friends, my measure of ills—
Fills my measure of woe;
Author was none, but I,
None other, of the blow;
For why was I to see,
When to descry
No sight on earth could have a charm for me?

1 SENATOR It was even as thou sayest.

OEDIPUS What was there left for sight?
What, that could give delight?
Or whose address,
O friends, could I still hear with happiness?
Lead me to exile straight;
Lead me, O my friends, the worst

Of murderers, of mortals most accurst,
Yea and to Gods chief object of their hate.

1 SENATOR Of cunning hapless, as of hapless fate,
I would that I had never known thy name!

OEDIPUS May he perish, whoe'er 'twas drew me
Out of the cruel gyve
That bound my feet, on the lea!
He who saved me alive,
Who rescued me from fate,
Shewing no kindness to me!
Sorrow so great,
Had I died then, had spared both mine and me.

1 SENATOR Fain were I too it had been so.

OEDIPUS Not then had I become
My father's murderer,
Nor wedded her I have my being from:
Whom now no God will bless,
Child of incestuousness
In her that bare me, being the spouse of her;
Yea if aught ill worse than all ill be there,
That Oedipus must bear.

1 SENATOR I know not how to say thou hast done well;
For it were better for thee now to die,
Than to live on in blindness.

OEDIPUS Tell me not—
Give me no counsel now, that what is done
Has not been done thus best. I know not how
With seeing eyes I could have looked upon
My father—coming to the under-world,
Or my poor mother, when against them both
I have sinned sins, worse than a halter's meed.
Or do you think that children were a sight
Delectable for me to gaze at, born

As they were born? Never with eyes of mine!
No, nor the city, nor the citadel,
Nor consecrated shrines of deities,
From which, to my most utter misery,
I, of all other men in Thebes the man
Most bravely nurtured, cut myself away,
And of my own mouth dictated to all
To thrust out me, the impious—me, declared
Abominable of Heaven, and Laius' son.
Was I, who in myself made evident
So dark a stain, with unaverted eyes
To look on these? That least of all! Nay rather,
If there were any way to choke the fount
Of hearing, through my ears, I would have tried
To seal up all this miserable frame
And live blind, deaf to all things; sweet it were
To dwell in fancy, out of reach of pain.
—Cithaeron! wherefore didst thou harbour me!
Why not at once have slain me? Never then
Had I displayed before the face of men
Who and from whom I am! O Polybus,
And Corinth, and the old paternal roof
I once called mine, with what thin film of honour,
Corruption over-skinned, you fostered me,
Found ill myself, and from ill parents, now!
O you, the three roads, and the lonely brake,
The copse, and pass at the divided way,
Which at my hands drank blood that was my own—
My father's—do you keep in memory
What in your sight I did, and how again
I wrought, when I came hither? Wedlock, wedlock,
You gave me being, you raised up seed again
To the same lineage, and exhibited
In one incestuous flesh son—brother—sire,
Bride, wife and mother; and all ghastliest deeds
Wrought among men! But O, ill done, ill worded!

In Heaven's name hide me with all speed away,
Or slay me, or send adrift upon some sea
Where you may look on me no longer! Come,
Touch, if you will, a miserable man;
Pray you, fear nothing; for my misery
No mortal but myself can underbear.

1 SENATOR Creon is at hand; he is the man you need,
Who must decide and do; being, after you,
The sole protector left us, for the land.

OEDIPUS Ah Heaven, what language shall I hold to him?
What rightful credit will appear in me?
For I have been found wholly in the wrong
In all that passed between us heretofore!

Enter CREON.

CREON Not as a mocker come I, Oedipus,
Nor to reproach for any former pain.
But you—even if you reverence no more
Children of men,—at least so far revere
The royal Sun-god's all-sustaining fire,
Not to parade, thus flagrant, such a sore
As neither earth nor day can tolerate,
Nor dew from Heaven! Take him in instantly!
That kindred only should behold and hear
The griefs of kin, fits best with decency.

OEDIPUS In Heaven's name, seeing that you transported me
Beyond all hope, coming, the first of men,
To me the last of men, grant me one boon!
'Tis for your good, not for my own, I say it.

CREON What is it that you crave so eagerly?

OEDIPUS Out of this country cast me with all speed,
Where I may pass without accost of men.

CREON So had I done, be sure, had I not wished
To learn our duty, first, at the God's mouth.

OEDIPUS Surely his oracle was all made plain,
Me, the profane, the parricide, to slay!

CREON So was it said; but in our present need
'Tis better to enquire what we must do.

OEDIPUS Will ye seek answer for a wretch like me?

CREON Even you might trust what the God answers, now.

OEDIPUS Ay, and I charge thee, and will beg of thee,
Order thyself such burial as thou wilt,
For her who lies within; seeing it is meet
Thou do so, for thine own. But never more
Be this my native town burdened with me
For living inmate; rather suffer me
To haunt the mountains—where my mountain is,
Cithaeron, which my mother and my sire,
Living, appointed for my sepulchre,
That as they meant, my slayers, I may expire.
Howbeit this much I know, neither disease
Nor aught beside can kill me; never else
Had I been rescued from the brink of death,
But for some dire calamity. Ah well,
Let our own fate wag onward as it may;
And for my sons, Creon, take thou no care
Upon thee; they are men, so that they never
Can lack the means to live, where'er they be;
But my two girls, wretched and pitiable,
For whose repast was never board of mine
Ordered apart, without me, but in all
That I partook they always shared with me,
Take care of them; and let me, above all else,
Touch them with hands, and weep away my troubles!
Pardon, my lord; pardon, illustrious sir;
If but my hands could feel them, I might seem
To have them still, as when I still could see.

ANTIGONE *and* ISMENE *are brought in.*

—What do I say? In Heaven's name, do I not
Hear my two darlings, somewhere shedding tears?
And can it be that Creon, pitying me,

Sends me my dearest, my two daughters, hither?
Is it so indeed?

CREON Yes, it is I vouchsafed this boon, aware
What joy you have and long have had of them.

OEDIPUS Why then, good luck go with thee, and Providence
Be guardian to thee, better than to me,
In payment for their coming!—Children dear,
Where are you? Come, come hither to my arms—
To these brotherly arms—procurers that
The eyes—that were your sire's—once bright—should see
Thus! who am shewn, O children, to have been
Author of you—unseeing—unknowing—in
Her bed, whence I derived my being! You
I weep for; for I cannot gaze on you;
Knowing what is left of bitter in the life
Which at men's hands you needs must henceforth live.
For to what gatherings of the citizens
Will you resort, or to what festivals,
Whence you will not, in place of holiday,
Come home in tears? Or when you shall have grown
To years of marriage, who—ah, who will be
The man to abide the hazard of disgrace
Such as must be the bane, both of my sons,
And you as well? For what reproach is lacking?
Your father slew his father, and became
Father of you—by her who bare him. So
Will they reproach you; who will wed you then?
No one, my children; but you needs must wither,
Barren—unwed. But thou, Menoeceus' son,
Since thou art all the father these have left them,
For we, the two that were their parents, now
Are both undone, do not thou suffer them
To wander, vagabond and husband-less,
Being of thy kin; nor let them fall so low
As are my fortunes; but have pity on them,
Seeing them so tender, and so desolate

Of all friends, but for thee. Give me thy hand,
Good sir, and promise this.—To you, my girls,
If you were old enough to understand,
I should have much to say; but as it is,
This be your prayer; in some permitted place
That you may breathe; and have your lot in life
Happier than his, who did engender you.

CREON Get thee in; thou hast bewailed thee enough, in reason.

OEDIPUS Though it be bitter, I must do it.

CREON All's good, in good season.

OEDIPUS Do you know how to make me?

CREON Say on, and I shall know.

OEDIPUS Banish me from this country.

CREON That must the God bestow.

OEDIPUS But to Gods, above all men, I am a mark for hate.

CREON And for that same reason you will obtain it straight.

OEDIPUS Say you so?

CREON Yes truly, and I mean what I say.

OEDIPUS Lead me hence then, quickly.

CREON Go; but let the children stay.

OEDIPUS Do not take them from me!

CREON Think not to have all at thy pleasure;
For what thou didst attain to far outwent thy measure.

CREON, *the Children, etc. retire.* OEDIPUS *is led in.*

Chorus.

Dwellers in Thebes, behold this Oedipus,
The man who solved the riddle marvellous,
A prince of men,
Whose lot what citizen
Did not with envy see,
How deep the billows of calamity
Above him roll.

Watch therefore and regard that supreme day;
And of no mortal say
"That man is happy," till
Vexed by no grievous ill
    He pass Life's goal.

[*Exeunt omnes.*